Notes
Gauraa Shekhar

word west press | brooklyn, new york

isbn: 978-1-7334663-6-3

published by word west in brooklyn, ny

first us edition 2023

printed in the usa

wordwest.co

cover & interior design: word west

And it's only doubts that we're counting
On fingers broken long ago
I read with every broken heart
We should become more adventurous

— "More Adventurous," Rilo Kiley

october	7
november	17
december	41
january	65
february	79
march	101
april	119

october

October 19, 2018 2:41 PM

buy toilet paper

October 19, 2018 2:47 PM

buy toilet paper and mixer

October 19, 2018 3:24 PM

my therapist told me i should stop indulging in self-deprecatory behavior like air quoting the word "writer" when i describe myself

October 19, 2018 7:18 PM

the poets are having another "we have so totally gathered here today" event at the bar and sarah is making me go i want to die

October 19, 2018 10:01 PM

poet with fedora inflicts upon me a ten-minute conversation re: his love for "shitty regional beer" then goes up to the bar and orders himself a miller lite

October 19, 2018 11:21 PM
game: drink every time a grad student ropes you into a conversation about the meaning of capital-a art

October 19, 2018 11:41 PM
ugh that girl with the jogger pants is here asking everyone at the bar what they're writing just waiting for the question to be asked back i think she's about to

October 19, 2018 11:47 PM
jogger pants doesn't ask me what i write about instead she announces with bold precision she's writing an essay collection about "the body"

October 19, 2018 11:49 PM
i think she bunny ears "the body" to beat everyone else from doing it first

October 20, 2018 12:24 AM
your friends at jack daniel's remind you to drink responsibly

October 20, 2018 1:23 AM
j.j. walks into the bar late his overgrown facial hair roaming into a goatee he kind of looks like guy fieri's duplicitous evil twin

October 20, 2018 1:27 AM
smoking a cigarette and manning another in my left hand i am the james salter of cigarettes

October 20, 2018 2:20 AM
"notorious" is a great film but so am i

October 20, 2018 4:18 AM
yellow light ydellow apartment yrlloqw braid very yellow

October 20, 2018 10:02 AM
~~um hi j.j. so the last text on my phone says "nobody breaks my fucking hbeart like you difd t o me" can u explain~~
~~hey j.j. it's me your panic pixie dream girl so like what went down last night can you elucidate the last thing i remember is pronouncing myself the james salter of cigarettes which made no sense then and makes even less sense now~~
~~do you maybe perhaps want to get a coffee at some point? don't really remember what transpired last night? and feel strange about it and wanted to clear the air?? it's really not a date!!~~
~~hey do you perhaps want to get a coffee at some point i don't really remember what transpired last night and feel strange about it and wanted to clear the air~~

October 21, 2018 3:13 PM
story idea: a tarot card reader who works at nokia

October 21, 2018 3:28 PM
buy fucking toilet paper

October 21, 2018 4:04 PM
i keep running into the guy who looks like

tom cruise if tom cruise were an inch shorter and had let himself go

October 22, 2018 6:45 PM
salinger had planned to go to indonesia did this ever come to fruition

October 23, 2018 9:56 AM
j.j. bought me plan b with his poker money well actually the poker money didn't cover it so he really used his credit card but on the walk back we decided that buying plan b with poker money was the better story

we went back to his place and he poured me water in a wine glass and i asked him if he remembered the time he bought me plan b with poker money we both laughed it was cute

October 24, 2018 8:03 PM
"no irish bars in this neighborhood!" someone cried

sarah cried too because she missed chicago where they have an irish pub on every corner sometimes i wish sarah loved chicago less

October 25, 2018 4:50 PM
story idea: your ex-boyfriend, let's call him cadfan, wakes up depressed and thinks of his ex's yellow-brown belly crisscrossed with stretchmarks and feels his cock pulsing against his briefs. he slips his hands inside and touches himself as he thinks of her tongue on his lips. he thinks of coming inside her, he thinks of spilling warm on her inner thigh and cries as he finishes and when

he opens his eyes he is in his childhood bedroom and the plush red dragon his parents bought him for his fifth birthday stares back at him in quiet judgment and then he smokes weed about it
       god this is so sad what if his parents are buying him weed that's so sad and they're like retired

October 26, 2018 10:08 AM
there are waxy takeout boxes in the trash from when i walked home hungover from j.j.'s and stopped at the overpriced italian deli

October 26, 2018 10:50 AM
can't decide if waking up with someone is better than falling asleep with someone not that i've done either of those things all week

October 26, 2018 11:14 AM
i'm always learning new things about myself in the most inconvenient ways

October 26, 2018 1:29 PM
if you're easy like sunday morning then j.j. is hard like the saturday morning that follows a night that didn't go according to plan

October 27, 2018 8:46 PM
they have string lights at the bar now were they always there

October 27, 2018 8:48 PM
the bartender just asked you when you're going to move in you need to stop coming here at least sometimes

October 28, 2018 8:28 AM
dreamt of a plane crash again
they couldn't find the debris the plane kept
going up and up and up

October 28, 2018 5:28 PM
sarah told me she ordered a candle that
smells like chicago, "like rich chocolate carried by
bursts of great lake michigan air"

October 28, 2018 5:29 PM
sometimes i wish somebody loved me as
much as sarah loves chicago

October 28, 2018 8:29 PM
story idea: unnamed narrator wears a short
satin dress and goes through life like she's gwen
stefani in the "cool" music video and rides a bike
everywhere but is very bad at it and she has a
very nice black coat

October 29, 2018 4:13 PM
story idea: boyfriend gets hit by a car before
she can break up with him
is it sad that i feel sadder for the fictional
girlfriend even though it's the guy who gets hit by
the car

October 30, 2018 11:13 AM
j.j.'s new way of asking me to sleep over is "do
you want to have a cigarette on my fire escape" and
i can't decide if that's more "breakfast at tiffany's" or
blink 182

October 30, 2018 11:19 AM
i know you're not supposed to bring a change of clothes when you're fucking casually but can you bring your contact lens case what's the protocol here

October 30, 2018 11:45 AM
every time i'm close to orgasm i think of the smell of the bakery across the street from day care

October 30, 2018 11:47 AM
"every time i'm close to orgasm i think of the smell of the bakery across the street from day care: and other abandonment issues"

October 30, 2018 1:09 PM
buy cigarettes and also toilet paper

October 30, 2018 5:32 PM
bosco really wants me to come to his halloween party and i'm not sure if it's because he likes me or because he's dressing as rita from mullholland drive but when he texted me that "all the boys are going to fall in love with him" i got a little bit jealous

October 31, 2018 10:01 PM
sarah and i showed up to bosco's party and bosco announced my name to the room
his roommate exclaimed and said bosco wouldn't shut up about me and we all looked at each other and then i looked at my shoes and asked where the bathroom is

October 31, 2018 10:29 PM
my friends are listening to dirty rap and throwing back picklebacks and i'm draining silver tequila out of this banana flask i am pretty sure is from hot topic

October 31, 2018 11:31 PM
whenever i tell bosco i might leave the party his face grows soft and he tries to pacify me by refilling my drink and taking the music playing phone from salena and handing it to me so i can play dj

October 31, 2018 11:37 PM
sarah is lying about smuggling cocaine again

October 31, 2018 11:41 PM
someone asked me what my halloween costume was and i wasn't in costume but i said "stacy's mom" and no one laughed

October 31, 2018 11:56 PM
sarah took two hits off a joint and held someone's costume stethoscope to her chest and said it wasn't working

October 31, 2018 11.58 PM
story idea: a narrative that consists solely of notes on an iphone

november

November 1, 2018 1:11 AM
bosco tried to kiss me as i helped him take his halloween makeup off and when i asked him if he had feelings for me he shook his head vehemently and said he just really likes me as a friend and it stung like a tepid slung of vodka

November 1, 2018 11:13 AM
haven't slept in my own bed in four days and still nobody wants me

November 1, 2018 11:43 AM
queens always feels bright and open when you're taking the train back to manhattan

November 1, 2018 12:18 PM
100% sure "wonderwall" is written about my hangover
my hangover is the high-pitched giggle at the beginning of "hungry like the wolf"
despite being often referred to as a one-hit wonder, my hangover landed me on the hot 100 four times in all

November 1, 2018 12:20 PM

my hangover is a ten hour loop of "africa" by toto

my hangover is the back of an empty cereal box
my hangover is the picture on the door of the refrigerator that's never stocked with food from "here comes a regular" by the replacements

November 1, 2018 4.58 PM

i am secretly happy that my friends are sad too

November 1, 2018 7.30 PM

i was drunk and eating a bagel last year last year i was drunk and eating a bagel last year when drunk i was eating a bagel when i was drunk, eating a bagel last year when i ate a bagel, i was drunk last year

November 2, 2018 8:35 AM

the jetsons was set in 2004

November 3, 2018 3:04 PM

it's 3 pm and i have lost track of time because i have been listening to "cool" by gwen stefani on repeat since 11 am

November 3, 2018 4:08 PM

my older friends are also falling apart

November 3, 2018 5:02 PM

sarah bet me that google knows who we're in love with and i told her i'm getting targeted ads about birth control

November 3, 2018 5:41 PM
in the trash are three condom wrappers and a love letter from an ex who is a rapper

November 3, 2018 9:55 PM
story idea: narrator doesn't know she's pregnant because she thinks she's been getting her period for four months but later finds out that she was spotting through her first trimester

November 4, 2018 9:59 AM
i was about to smoke a cigarette but i reached for the lighter in my pocket and realized it was j.j.'s and then i was like what if the cadfan story ends with him watching a girl walk away with someone else in the rain and then when he reaches for his lighter he finds that it's his ex's lighter and it makes him sad because sometimes people leave things behind when they leave you
we are all the sum of the lighters we accidentally end up pocketing

November 4, 2018 10:34 AM
buy toilet paper

November 4, 2018 11:16 PM
overheard at party: how are we going to be gay in l.a. if we have no money to get to l.a.

November 5, 2018 11:16 AM
real life cadfan sent me a double album he wrote after the breakup and we made a drinking game out of it and drank every time my name was referenced in a rap and every time there was

a death threat pointed at j.j. and we drank when he said "you light up my life like amphros" for no reason other than it was bad and tragic in a very special way

sarah remarked he does that dumb british thing where he sounds like he's crying

November 6, 2018 11:30 AM
tis the season to be hit on in the whole foods vegan aisle before 12 pm

November 7, 2018 5:36 PM
remember when you thought smoking pot would help you write a story without being sad all the time but all you did was write to the music video for "cool" by gwen stefani and by "write" i mean scribble the line "her nose creases and crumples like the wrapper of a candy bar" on the back of a duane reade receipt

November 7, 2018 5:38 PM
remember when you stole your mom's xanax and watched "the sure thing" and dreamt about not remembering sex instead that was real fun

November 8, 2018 10:04 AM
fell asleep with my contacts in because i wanted to give my body—the somatic!—the feeling of waking up with a boy

November 9, 2018 10:47 PM
i die where my money lives: an alternative title for tobias wolff's "bullet in the brain"

November 10, 2018 9:09 AM

i don't want to write this story about this guy jacking off and crying at the same time it makes me sad and i don't want to be sad also i just spent two hours changing 'dick' to 'cock' and then back to 'dick' only to change it to 'cock' again

November 10, 2018 11:12 AM

story idea: what if after jacking off and crying cadfan hears his parents calling for him over the sound of the kettle whistling and tinny teaspoons against the rims of teacups and when he goes downstairs for tea his mom's like "i think you need to brush your teeth, maybe"

November 10, 2018 6:22 PM

texted dad "writing is hard" to which he replied "is this about a boy"

November 10, 2018 6:26 PM

don't sleep with j.j. again he likes you, he does, but he also likes cocaine and last night he spent two hours watching guy fieri on tv and you hung out till 3 in the morning waiting for him to come down

also he looks too much like guy fieri

November 10, 2018 6:30 PM

what if in the story after cadfan comes/cries he thinks about his ex-girlfriend and how she spelled jinx with a 'y' like 'jynx' and always played the beach boys when it rained

November 10, 2018 6:45 PM

i don't want to be alone tonight i just want to cry into someone's arms being with someone won't necessarily make me less lonely or sad though

November 10, 2018 6:48 PM

story idea: what if cadfan, after the expulsion of various bodily fluids, gets really high and stares intently at a date through a restaurant window and what if he stares so hard without even realizing that they notice and move tables

fuck that's so goddamn depressing

November 10, 2018 7:05 PM

story idea: cadfan tastes the salt leaking from his eyes he feels the spill on his stomach hears tim and sally talking about retirement and walks to his dresser and he's out of tissues so he uses the towel and then shuffles through the folders of pokémon cards to retrieve the weed hal scored for him from cardiff he scissors through the skunky green brown and rolls himself a joint and smokes it while studying the sheep in the field across the house and wonders if they know what's coming for them

November 10, 2018 7:53 PM

getting older just means it gets marginally easier every year to stow your depression in the junk drawer

November 11, 2018 11:04 AM

j.j. and i were out in public just the two of us and he ordered us a bottle of red wine and i told him about the time my mom took me on a train to see my grandparents when i was seven and she said we were just going there for the weekend but when we got there she was like haha we're staying here for a whole year and also i'm fucking my brother in law

was that a date

November 11, 2018 11:24 AM
on the walk back home, stepped into a puddle and thought about cum

November 11, 2018 4:09 PM
j.j. now knows you have condoms in your wallet but does he know how long they've been there

November 11, 2018 4:10 PM
he lent me his copy of "pale fire" to read
nabokov! not sure which one of us wears the daddy issues now

November 11, 2018 4:13 PM
what are the romantic implications of him kissing my forehead in the morning is he in love with me yet jk

November 11, 2018 6:17 PM
it makes sarah uncomfortable that i keep calling airplane bottles "nips" so i try and say "nips" doubly as often now

November 11, 2018 6:18 PM
bagging nips and bringing them in to tom's so we can dip sweet potato fries into spiked coffee

November 11, 2018 6:19 PM

we got kicked out of tom's not because of the nips or the spiked coffee but because we were on our laptops

November 11, 2018 8:54 PM

today sarah categorized her type as someone who is 1. midwestern and 2. knows her name
asked her what she thinks my type is and she did not pause to think before declaring "moderately reformed teenage dirtbag"

November 12, 2018 12:01 AM

sarah is describing the smell of chicago to bosco

November 12, 2018 2:09 AM

bosco asked me if i thought the government was keeping track of me via lipstick stained cigarette butts

November 12, 2018 10:42 AM

someone posted an ultrasound of their un- born baby on fb
i had a panic attack as j.j. left my apartment last night you don't see me bragging about it

November 13, 2018 12:13 PM

my therapist said i have "great issues" was that a compliment, or

November 13, 2018 1:22 PM

remember how in the season one finale of the o.c. marissa watches ryan drive away from the curb, his bike in the trunk of the car, and she realizes he's leaving for chino and he realizes that

she realizes he's leaving and he looks back and
they make eye contact and ryan lifts his hand to
form a stagnant russell crowe wave goodbye and
she just watches him disappear and jeff buckley's
cover of "hallelujah" smudges the air
    that would never happen between me and j.j.
j.j. would never look back

November 13, 2018 1:36 PM

lovers from door to bed
strangers from bed to door

November 13, 2018 1:45 PM

people are always concerned about my protein
intake when they find out i'm vegan and i'm like
hello i love nuts

November 13, 2018 9:29 PM

they were playing "i'm like a bird" at mcdonald's
and i realized i'm less like a bird who only flies away
and more like a city pigeon who'd much rather be
kicked in the chest than leave

November 14, 2018 10:13 AM

i always keep my watch on during sex not
sure what that means

November 14, 2018 11:17 AM

sarah told me i should probably stop having
boys over when bosco is sleeping on my couch
and i told her that's not the case because bosco
explicitly told me he only likes me as a friend
    i didn't tell her that he kept reaching for my
hand at the bar all night

November 14, 2018 1:07 PM
i developed feelings and now i'm inflicting death upon them

November 14, 2018 9:56 PM
can't tell your parents about your drinking habit even though you saw your mom cut her finger on the ceiling fan dancing on a chair when you were five

November 15, 2018 10:09 AM
woke up with a pecan in my bed and ate it

November 15, 2018 10:11 PM
sarah is talking about chicago again sarah is upset not because kanye west named his daughter chicago west but because he named his daughter chicago west when he's really from oak lawn and everyone knows oak lawn "isn't really chicago"

November 15, 2018 11:34 PM
dad asked me what's a casual relationship like i knew the answer

November 16, 2018 12:03 AM
when real life cadfan asked you for your password and you told him it was hellokitty666 he embraced you in a way that was quietly inti-mate, more intimate than a kiss and he looked at you the same way j.j. looked at you when you were out on the fire escape just the two of you and the cigarette ashed on your new tights with red roses splattered across and it burnt a

hole in them and you exclaimed and j.j. asked if you were ok and you said you were more upset about the tights and j.j. threw his arms around you and kissed your forehead in a way that felt tender and right as if to say hey maybe you're one of my kind

November 16, 2018 9:32 AM
buy:
toilet paper
facial wipes
candles that smell like fresh linen and not chicago

November 16, 2018 11:43 AM
dreamt about j.j. again in the dream i told him i was pregnant and he said i would have to take care of it myself but he can bring me a banana if i would like
when i woke up i thought about how i don't remember what his novel is about but still have papercuts from the manuscript

November 16, 2018 11:54 AM
my older friends are always falling apart

November 16, 2018 2:44 PM
wish i was as committed to doing laundry as i am to drinking silver tequila

November 16, 2018 4:57 PM
j.j. told me if real life cadfan were jesus i would be his mankind

November 16, 2018 6:13 PM

remember being on a "water cleanse" the summer you were with brendon and when he lost his job at the bank the two of you got chinese and he watched you pick each floret of broccoli off the plate and bring it to your red mouth he said it was the first time he watched you eat

November 16, 2018 6:30 PM

shrinking yourself to zero because disappearing is a great way to get attention

November 17, 2018 8:27 AM

story idea: cadfan is at a bar in aberystwyth wales messaging his ex and when she doesn't respond he scrolls through her old facebook pictures and remembers the times she'd been bigger and smaller and it makes him sick to know she's being held by someone who didn't even know all the people she was before

November 17, 2018 4:35 PM

from joe jackson's "is she really going out with him?" to sophie b. hawkins' "damn! i wish i was your lover": a love story in five stages of kübler-ross denial

November 17, 2018 9:25 PM

can't tell your parents about your drinking habit even though you walked into the bathroom when you were six and saw your aunt with her fingers down your mom's throat in the tub

November 18, 2018 11:04 AM
xanax was developed first for dogs

November 18, 2018 9:10 PM
finally decided to unpack the box with the ceramic wine goblets that real life cadfan's uncle mick sculpted for my family and i thought about cadfan the real one and i thought about that christmas in wales and that godawful scrawny christmas tree his family grew in their garden and carried over to their living room in a red pot on christmas eve and we roasted chestnuts by the fire and sang carols and tried not to think about putting the beloved family cat down after the car came for him and i held real life cadfan as he cried and that night i let him come inside

November 18, 2018 10:12 PM
i've never dated anyone who didn't have a brother

November 18, 2018 10:27 PM
real life cadfan's parents sometimes added honey to their tea but were vegan for the most part they had a compost bin and owned lou reed's transformer on vinyl and good books lined their inexpensive but nice shelves and i felt like i could talk to them about anything i think i miss them more than i miss cadfan i miss being inducted into another family

November 18, 2018 4:32 PM
sarah and i were bored so we decided to throw a party

November 18, 2018 5:15 PM
driving to target to pick up beer and string lights because we are so fun and adventurous

November 18, 2018 5:34 PM
asked sarah if i should invite both j.j. and bosco to the party she said every decision i make is the right decision for me

November 18, 2018 6:01 PM
texted j.j. we are having a party and he asked "if the crew should roll through" then added "the crew being myself" i thought it was cute

November 18, 2018 9:19 PM
j.j. keeps asking me if i wanna have a cigarette on the fire escape but he also keeps disappearing into different corners of the party

November 18, 2018 9:50 PM
salena shows up to the party with two bottles of grey goose yelling shots! shots! shots! then tells the room how she's worried about money

November 18, 2018 10:11 PM
sometimes i feel like i confess to truths i don't believe

November 18, 2018 11:14 PM
sarah keeps leavisg apartment to dowbdstairs have cigaettes with natty even thoe evreryone's smoking in the apartment she keeops foretting that th e music is conncted her phone

November 19, 2018 12:49 AM
bosco is telldng me i should go t o bes d but thi s is fmy home

November 19, 2018 12:58 AM
wanted a cig someon e stole my cigratees from thye window sill

November 19, 2018 10:18 AM
~~hey j.j. i know i was drunk and kind of fucked up last night but i don't understand how you could say all those things to me call me beautiful take care of me clean up the apartment and just leave while i was freaking out having a panic attack and begging you to stay~~
~~hey j.j. i'm not sure how to feel right now should i feel moved because you cleaned up my apartment and made everyone leave or should i feel hurt because you left me in the middle of a panic attack~~

November 19, 2018 10:33 AM
hey j.j. i'm sorry about last night i'm sure i was a lot and i was probably just feeling a lot of things considering the quantities consumed i just wanted to make sure we were cool

November 19, 2018 1:04 PM
buy toilet paper

November 19, 2018 1:42 PM
casual means he will kiss your forehead on the fire escape and clean your apartment after the

party but leave while you're having a panic attack

November 19, 2018 2:58 PM
maybe i don't like boys as much as i don't like sleeping alone

November 19, 2018 7:03 PM
asked the playlist "what does it mean when a boy tells you he likes you but deserts you minutes later while you're having a panic attack" and then hit shuffle hoping that the song would answer my question

"he could be the one," the playlist answered

November 20, 2018 8:21 PM
story idea: girl with autophobia puts herself in dangerous situations in order to avoid sleeping alone and no one suspects anything because she's social and people seem to want to be around her but secretly she spends too much time distrusting that barbara streisand song about people who need people because she doesn't think people who need people are the luckiest people

November 20, 2018 9:48 PM
realized my mom also had anxiety sleeping alone and so did my grandmother and so did my aunt so i called mom and told her about the panic attack and asked her why she was so terrified and i half expected her to unpack a longstanding tradition of inherited trauma but instead she told me she was scared of ghosts

November 20, 2018 10:02 PM
my mom makes horror films for a living but is scared of ghosts

November 20, 2018 10:20 PM
can't tell your parents about your drinking habit even though they gave you rum and coke when you asked for pepsi after soccer practice and you spat it out on your mom's feet
she never wore shoes indoors

November 20, 2018 11:13 PM
me: it's almost the weekend let's get drunk
friends who aren't sarah and bosco: um it's tuesday

November 20, 2018 11:38 PM
natty said that calling his power move a power move is a power move

November 21, 2018 10:52 AM
queued "killer queen" by queen at karaoke when sarah told me the song was written about a prostitute
maybe on some level all my childhood traumas stem from a base misunderstanding of the song "killer queen" by queen

November 21, 2018 11:14 AM
julia roberts has the best forehead vein of all time

November 22, 2018 1:42 AM
if the thrill of the chase is tater tots then the

hurt and anxiety are the charred and burnt bits of batter you find at the bottom of the serving tray that you eat anyway because you're hungry and they're there and you hope they might not be as charred and burnt as they look

November 22, 2018 2:31 AM
story idea: two people in a casual relationship accidentally spend thanksgiving together because the weather is no good and they stay in and eat tofurkey from trader joe's and they smoke up and shuffle through the channels on tv and a voice on nat geo says "for most animals here, the food is critically balanced and the lure of easy pickings might have driven them there" and they laugh until they kiss and then the guy half jokingly asks her if she thinks they're a delicate food chain to which she responds "what do you think it feels like to suck out someone's bone marrow"

November 22, 2018 6:31 AM
dreamt of beached turtles and romaine

November 22, 2018 9:12 AM
j.j. bends time and you fold into it and everything is still and long

November 22, 2018 10:44 AM
i used to swallow but i'm vegan now

November 22, 2018 10:47 AM
casual means he will tell you he has feelings for you but repeatedly state his need to sleep in his own bed while you're in the midst of a panic attack at 3 am

November 23, 2018 7:42 PM
there's a brick on sarah's fire escape and i'm drowning slowly

November 24, 2018 11:29 AM
story idea: a breakup text that reads "i feel asphyxiated by your lowercase letters" and nothing more

November 24 2018 12.01 PM
never not thinking about the time j.j. told me women shouldn't put out until the third date because reward is a primal need for men
we went home together the night we first met

November 25, 2018 11:32 PM
casual means he will not check in on you after the panic attack or wish you on thanksgiving but will ask the group chat if they'd be down to microdose acid and write flash fiction

November 26, 2018 2:32 AM
growing up is realizing they will only like you while you're novelty sputtering pop gutter trash in bright red lipstick and a lowcut dress

November 26, 2018 9:52 AM
buy toilet paper not the recycled kind again please

November 26, 2018 11:26 AM
~~j.j. i know i said we were cool in the morning but we're not cool and it's not cool and life is not "cool" by gwen stefani and i can be fun and~~

~~funny but the moment i start having real human~~
~~emotions you feel the need to sleep in your own~~
~~bed~~

November 27, 2018 10:42 PM
putting on makeup and a credit card dress to feel somewhat roughly new because sometimes that's just what you gotta do

November 27, 2018 11:27 PM
sarah told me my lipstick stains remind her of dried blood

November 28, 2018 2:36 AM
sometimes i feel like hilary duff trapped in the body of lindsay lohan except i don't have the body of lindsay lohan

November 28, 2018 4:23 AM
dreamt i was ten again and mom was stuffing packs of marlboro lights into a blender to make me a nicotine breakfast smoothie

November 29, 2018 1:39 PM
sarah wrapped a slice of tofu in a napkin and asked me to pass her a book because she read on the internet that pressing tofu down makes it taste better so i handed her norman mailer's "the armies of the night"

November 29, 2018 1:43 PM
does tofu taste different when it is pressed with norman mailer

November 29, 2018 11:13 PM
2018 and i'm still trying to "solve" boys by listening to the cure

November 30, 2018 4:12 PM
sometimes i feel less like a writer and more like a character upon whom extenuating circumstances are inflicted to keep ratings high

december

December 02, 2018 12:13 PM
because j.j. has a trust fund and a mayflower
family and his mother is a daughter of the american
revolution and because he dresses like his parents
dressed him exclusively in osh kosh b'gosh and
he never took the measures to self correct and
because he's from connecticut and has commit-
ment issues i thought it made him exactly like the
less hot version of logan huntzberger from gilmore
and i thought when i would show up at his door
after spending the night on sarah's bathroom floor
and tell him it's all or nothing he would say it's all
are you kidding of course it's all but instead he got
me drunk and grabbed the condoms he knew were
in my wallet and fucked me while i was asleep and
didn't notice or care that i was crying and in the
morning he kissed my forehead and said let's go
ahead and never do this again

December 04, 2018 9:08 AM
buy toilet paper

December 03, 2018 10:54 AM
buy fucking toilet paper just do it

December 05, 2018 6:36 PM
nothing left in the fridge so i ate the laxative chocolate regretted that at 5:09 AM, 10:03 AM and 6:36 PM

December 06, 2018 11:31 PM
told natty that j.j. has a color swatch and he once told me that he could never be with someone darker than a certain shade of brown and natty told me that the daughters of the american revolution refused to let marian anderson use constitution hall because she was black and there was a white artist only clause printed in every contract

December 08, 2018 5:53 AM
~~um hey i have been thinking about this and it wasn't cool that you fucked me while i was asleep and it wasn't cool that i was too drunk to move and crying and you didn't care and you knew i liked you and you kissed me on the forehead and said let's never do this again and it's not cool that you used the word ogle in the context of another woman's naked body like five minutes after it was not cool not ok and i want you to know i am a human being who grew up and watched tv and had interests and a myspace account and when i was four i wrote a song called "i wish i could fly" and my parents were proud and made me sing it~~

~~when they had friends over and it was different~~
~~every time and sometimes seven minutes long~~
~~and it was so dumb and it rhymed and they were~~
~~still so proud and did you know when i was six i~~
~~wanted to be a painter and did you know that i~~
~~wanted to be an opera singer when i was fifteen~~
~~because i fell in love with maria callas her voice~~
~~felt like falling down the stairs and did you know~~
~~that i couldn't get myself to swear until i was~~
~~eighteen and i flinched every time i said the word~~
~~fuck till i was nineteen and i had a life before you~~
~~saw me standing at the bar in the red dress with~~
~~the chinese collar and i thought i could never get~~
~~with a guy who looks like guy fieri and you broke~~
~~my things you broke the condom you broke the~~
~~wine glass you broke my phone screen and made~~
~~my fingers bleed too and did you know the doctor~~
~~told me it could've been ectopic and as i sat in the~~
~~chair waiting i decided i shouldn't text you before~~
~~i knew for sure because you'd think i was being~~
~~melodramatic you always confuse understandable~~
~~rage for female hysteria~~
~~hey i have been thinking about this and it~~
~~wasn't cool, what happened, and i was crying~~
~~and you didn't seem to care and you didn't seem~~
~~sorry but you voted for gary johnson so i guess~~
~~that makes me the moron who should've seen this~~
~~coming~~
~~fuck you but not literally~~
~~please give sarah back my things p.s. you're~~
~~uninvited to my party~~

December 08, 2018 1:09 PM
dreamt of slugs

December 08, 2018 4.56 PM
~~j.j. i have a family that worries and friends who love me too much to let me make excuses for you~~

December 09, 2018 3:53 PM
i think i am one nervous breakdown from collaging

December 09, 2018 6:27 PM
resent sarah for making me leave the apartment but love sarah for getting mcdonald's delivered to the bar

December 09, 2018 8:45 PM
bosco told me he always feels like everyone is going to abandon him and then sometimes he feels like he does it to himself and then he's weirdly relieved when someone actually abandons him because he can be all like haha i was right
sometimes i wish i were less optimistic too

December 09, 2018 10:53 PM
sarah asked me why i don't walk on the right side of the sidewalk and i was like the first sidewalk i ever saw was on vacation sarah we didn't all grow up in chicago

December 10, 2018 8:57 AM
dreamt of slugs and dogwood

December 10, 2018 9:16 AM
thought i saw a flurry but it was just ash from the cigarette

December 10, 2018 4:08 PM

natty told me no man who owns a knee length leather jacket didn't vote for gary johnson

December 10, 2018 8:56 PM

i like to eat food with a teaspoon so that it lasts longer but also because it makes me feel smaller

December 10, 2018 9:31 PM

i'm sitting next to the table where j.j. and i drank two bottles of wine and i told him about the time my mom took me on a train to see my grandparents and told me she was fucking her brother in law

there's another couple drinking wine there now and i'm not sure if i should feel as sad or sad at all because of what he did

December 10, 2018 9:36 PM

like i don't know can you mourn the people you thought people used to be without making excuses for their actions in the present

December 12, 2018 2:23 AM

your friends at jack daniel's remind you to drink responsibly

December 12, 2018 7:46 AM

sometimes i wonder about what i look like in other people's dreams

December 12, 2018 9:31 AM

called up real life cadfan and told him what

happened because i thought he was the only boy
capable of being nice to me and i cried and he
cried and he told me all straight men are predatory
around "beauty and vulnerability" including him
and then he blocked my number

December 12, 2018 10:28 AM
ran into j.j. today he fledged his guy fieri goatee
into a seventies wishbone pornstache he jerked his
chin up to 'sup me and i said nothing

December 12, 2018 10:33 AM
almond
milk
creamer
bananas
spinach
tofu
noodles
hot sauce soy
candles
mushrooms
coconut milk
green curry

December 12, 2018 11:07 AM
walked up and down twenty blocks for no reason
other than i wanted "cool" by gwen stefani to stay
constantly in motion

December 12, 2018 11:32 AM
told bosco i was sorry for being sad and then
he said don't be sorry we're all sad all the time
and sent me pictures of chickens

to dos:
cancel new yorker subscription
learn to be alone

December 12, 2018 11:41 AM

December 12, 2018 9:40 PM
tried to lock my door the same way i would
my parents' door maybe i miss them more than i
let myself think

December 12, 2018 10:03 PM
realized i hadn't heard the sound of dad's
voice since august so i called him but he declined
every time and eventually responded with "sorry
busy"
men will ghost you regardless of age and
relation

December 12, 2018 10:46 PM
my room is dark except for the glow of the
neighbors' christmas lights

December 14, 2018 11:49 AM
every cloud has a yellow legal pad lining

December 14, 2018 1:59 PM
sarah is throwing me a party on account of my
"half birthday" i suspect her last ditch effort to make
me leave my apartment is inviting the city inside
she said she would pick up beer and even let
me pick the music

December 14, 2018 10:59 PM
sarah strung a christmas bulb necklace around me and requested "chicago" by sufjan stevens at the party

December 14, 2018 11:05 PM
elliot is drunkenly recommending a lot of podcasts he said podcasts are like the news minus huey lewis which ok i admit is a little funny

December 14, 2018 11:41 PM
we were on the fire escape and i ran out of cigarettes and elliot bummed me an american spirit and it was cold so he lent me his coat and bosco squirmed a little and said he needed to go home

December 15, 2018 12:09 AM
sarah set up the projector for karaoke and salena screamed "total eclipse of the heart" into the karaoke mic interjecting "fucking" in place of each "really" like that scene from "old school" and the downstairs neighbors knocked at the door and shut down the party

December 15, 2018 12:23 AM
searched the apartment for bosco but he was already gone

December 15 2018 1:14 AM
drank the last can of bud light on the table it was lukewarm

December 15, 2018 2:21 AM

~~hey bosco it sucks that you disappeared tonight without saying anything and it sucks that things between us feel very distant now and it's been a rough week for me and you haven't been here you haven't even asked me how i've been coping it would be nice to be considered i feel like it would've been nice to have been considered i could've used some support but you're just amiss~~

December 15, 2018 2:25 AM

hey bosco thanks for coming tonight but it sucks that you left without saying anything and it sucks that things feel distant and it sucks that you never asked me how i've been coping i thought we were friends it sucks that my life is on fire and i'm supposed to get drunk and wrap myself up in christmas lights as a distraction

December 15, 2018 6:59 AM

woke up to a string of missed calls and apologetic texts from bosco he said he was my family and he's going to be there for me and is taking the train back to manhattan and when i opened my apartment door at six in the morning he was asleep in the lobby with his head resting on his backpack

December 16, 2018 9:40 PM

mom told me she was going to send my christmas present early this year and she put a lot of thought into it i waited for the package eagerly and opened it at the bar with bosco and

elliot
it was a copy of michelle obama's 'becoming'
and three bottles of cetaphil face wash for sensitive
skin

December 17, 2018 2:49 PM
sarah is flying home for christmas before she
left she gave me a copy of her keys and a ticket to
chicago because she didn't want either me or her
apartment to get lonely over break

December 17, 2018 4:08 PM
think i finally figured out why i don't like that
sarah loves chicago: it's not right it's not fair not to
be bitter about where you come from

December 17, 2018 5:38 PM
bosco and elliot and i ordered chinese and
watched a b grade horror movie about a guy in a
cabin stalked by a videographer

December 17, 2018 5:40 PM
after elliot left we watched gilmore girls and
bosco laughed so hard when mrs kim said "boys
don't like funny girls" and when he reached out for
my hand i let him

December 18, 2018 9:31 PM
fiona called me up and said i have to come
to tampa for her wedding reception she wouldn't
take no for an answer and tickets will be booked
whether i like it for not

December 18, 2018 11:01 PM

told bosco i love my friends i do but suddenly i feel like everybody's favorite charity case

December 19, 2018 1:20 PM

bosco squinted like a dog when i told him i would be leaving soon he said his roommates were already prepping a vegan spread for christmas

December 20, 2018 7:28 AM

after four months of following me of coming when called of telling me not to sleep with j.j. of sleeping on the couch while i was in bed with other men after four months of persisting i told bosco i liked him too and then he was like i do like you but i really like hanging out with you and you're my favorite person in the program and a part of me died because i thought he'd cite the lyrics to "she's so high" by tal b but he didn't instead he also rejected me

December 20, 2018 1:33 PM

sex: the quickest way to dissolve a friendship

December 21, 2018 9:26 PM

my old boss sexts me and i get drunk enough to sext him back but mostly try to veer the conversation toward elliott smith and his wife's first trimester

December 21, 2018 10:47 PM

sarah said pick the nice guy the right guy the kind of guy who makes time for you who wants to be with you

December 21, 2018 10:50 PM
my old boss told me i'm intense and so i attract men who are intense and sometimes that's a bad thing but that shouldn't stop me from caring about someone

December 21, 2018 11:48 PM
fiona texted me "to get the fuck off the couch you don't need to be watching 'he's just not that into you' for a third time"

December 22, 2018 7:28 AM
the worst part is that i didn't find bosco attractive or alluring his face flakes in the morning and he's not very tall and he strides funny and wears hideous scarves his only selling point was that he was genuinely nice and into me and now he's not even that and now the friendship is ruined i just don't understand

December 22, 2018 8:18 AM
not sure what's lower the bar or my self esteem

December 23, 2018 10:12 PM
matthew mcconaughey, a pathological flirt?

December 23, 2018 10:29 PM
my old boss told me he saw jenny lewis open for elliott smith the year before elliott smith died he also told me he ran into jenny at a grocery store in echo park

December 23, 2018 10:40 PM
held myself back from typing "i miss you" am
i finally guarded now

December 24, 2018 8:21 AM
my holiday mood is taking long blurry walks
down amsterdam ave in the middle of a snowstorm
without contacts in listening to "does he love you?"
by rilo kiley

December 24 2018 8.26 AM
maybe the best outcome for someone like me
is to end up in california with a married man the
wind on my back and the sun on my face

December 24, 2018 8:31 AM
he'll promise to leave his wife for me and
maybe he'll send me letters in the mail twice a
week until he won't anymore because he'd never
actually leave his wife for me

December 24, 2018 8:39 AM
merry christmas or whatever i guess

December 24, 2018 3:02 PM
before i got on the plane to tampa bosco wished
me a safe flight and asked me to text him when i
land
is this like the episode of my so called life where
jordan catalano realizes he loves angela chase

December 24, 2018 3:06 PM
not sure if i'm jordan catalano or angela
chase in this equation

December 24, 2018 8:27 PM
one hour in tampa and of course i've already met a dog named bosco

December 24, 2018 8:40 PM
apparently catfish country has the best gator bites

December 24, 2018 11:18 PM
got to fiona's family home and walked into a weed cloud and signed andy warhol prints lined the walls and there was a gumball machine and a jukebox and gaudy mismatched pieces of seventeenth century furniture there were ramones coasters and clash records and there was a modest pool in the backyard a kind of pool that suggested they had the kind of money that could afford cristal but was spent on retsina instead
i wished this were my family home

December 25, 2018 8:27 AM
christmas morning in tampa begins with a chilled tecate and ends with a j

December 25, 2018 9:03 AM
cocktail olives and artichokes for breakfast because gator bites aren't vegan

December 25, 2018 9:29 AM
misremembering lyrics to stacy's mom is a very specific kind of embarrassing

December 25, 2018 10:06 AM
fiona's dad tosses the keys to his black six circuit ferrari batmobile and fiona's husband andel who doesn't have a license catches them i'm not sure if we'll make it to christmas lunch

December 25, 2018 10:11 AM
the car swerved on the highway and i got scared and i texted the group chat with sarah and bosco i told them i love them i forgot to text my family
money makes you shallow build a moat buy a boat

December 25, 2018 2:28 PM
they served beef for lunch so i drank coke instead

December 25, 2018 3:27 PM
fiona's dad pulled up a new york post article about a woman who had sex with twenty ghosts and is now engaged to a spirit and i don't know i really felt that
my first crush was casper the friendly ghost because he couldn't be bad or mean or alive

December 25, 2018 4:16 PM
joey said he'd totally be the guy who has sexual intercourse with twenty sandwiches and then gets engaged to a rueben
i like that for him

December 25, 2018 6:21 PM
christmas in tampa is just us driving from one

million dollar home to another million dollar home
with literal moats

December 25, 2018 7:43 PM
there was nothing i could eat on the table so
fiona's dad volunteered to make me something
and i felt so bad i almost ate the chicken out of
politeness

December 25, 2018 7:58 PM
spilling wine on the million dollar kitchen
flooring i felt so bad that fiona lit me another j

December 25, 2018 8:13 PM
is it bad that i can't stop thinking about how
fiona's grandmother cut her a check for 5k
like i got a twenty dollar bill from my aunt

December 25, 2018 8:26 PM
literally not sure if my grandmother even has
my number

December 26, 2018 9:12 PM
the color scheme in the shining defines my
wardrobe

December 26, 2018 9:23 PM
i am shelly duvall in the shining
smoking, crying

December 26, 2018 10:34 PM
elliot texted me a link to a key and peele
sketch about "baby it's cold outside"

December 26, 2018 10:39 PM
i want you to go it's cold inside

December 26, 2018 11:01 PM
joey said an existential crisis is like diarrhea
it could happen at any time

December 26, 2018 11:27 PM
fiona got stoned and told me about the time
her sister asked her to drive her to a walmart
because she needed tampons but really her sister
just wanted to look at guns because she thought
the scientologists were after her fiona talked her
out of it but not before she tried to push her into
the trout lake

December 26, 2018 11:34 PM
texted natty about this because i was concerned
he said you can't get a quality gun at a walmart your
money is better spent somewhere else support your
local business

December 26, 2018 11:53 PM
real life cadfan called me up and i answered
thinking it was to wish me merry christmas but
instead he told me he was moving to japan to teach
english because of something i once said to him

December 27, 2018 7:01 PM
dreamt i was caught pissing in a dog bowl in
my kitchen

December 27, 2018 8:27 PM
driving back from bartow and fiona points to

the sheds that line the highway casually saying oh
hey these used to be very famous meth houses

December 27, 2018 10:19 PM
call me lime-o-rita ora
honey i zombie flipp'd the house honey i
zombie flipp'd the kids

December 27, 2018 10:54 PM
"careless hipsters" by george michael

December 27, 2018 11:12 PM
always refer to dancing as jiving the menace
of marijuana

December 28, 2018 8:38 AM
dreamt bosco kissed me again
also dreamt i was a gay witch tripping acid at
a warehouse party in brooklyn

December 29, 2018 12:10 AM
ask
rick steves
instead of ask jeeves

December 29, 2018 3:59 AM
fiona said oasis should get back together and
write an antiwall wonderwall

December 29, 2018 4:07 AM
everyone i looked up to when i was sixteen
was as old as i am today

December 29, 2018 4:31 AM

don't know why but i always think kate moss is dead i think it's just because i want her to be dead so she can be a tragic figure

December 29, 2018 10:37 PM

cock daddy said joey to the rusty rooster

December 29, 2018 10:45 PM

fiona just waved to the guy smoking down al's barbeque

December 29, 2018 11:08 PM

the dj at the karaoke bar refused to play "closing time" because it was too early

December 29, 2018 11:21 PM

fiona and i drank too much and sat on the porch smoking american spirits and listening to britney spears and she told me she wished she hadn't gotten married

December 29, 2018 11:32 PM

the only moral code in tampa is not playing closing time by semisonic before closing time

December 30, 2018 3:17 PM

my life is like a cw finale where there's a wedding reception or a party of some kind and we're all so well dressed but there's something on my mind something secretly brewing

December 30, 2018 5:54 PM

fiona is dressed as lauren bacall in "how to

marry a millionaire" she got me a black veil to match

December 30, 2018 7:44 PM
guy in top hat named alex compliments my nose ring and asks me about my new year's resolution only to tell me his is doing more push ups

December 30, 2018 7:53 PM
alex trying to get to know me is interrupting me trying to get to know my martini glass

December 30, 2018 8:06 PM
told alex i'm kinda drunk because the only vegan food here is the olive juice in this martini he said he can count on his hand the number of drinks i cut him off to say he doesn't sound drunk he said he can count on his hands the number of drinks he's had in his lifetime

December 30 2018 8.09 PM
learned alex is christian and practicing

December 30, 2018 8:14 PM
alex forked the amaretto icing off the wedding cake because he "had to drive home" 34

December 30, 2018 8:28 PM
and the only thing we had in common at the table is that none of us consented to being alive

December 31, 2018 11:17 AM
i am hangover hash

December 31, 2018 3:12 PM
i write sins not tragedies and that's a tragedy

December 31, 2018 3:20 PM
bosco asked me to text me after i land safely in chicago does this mean he likes me again

December 31, 2018 8:16 PM
settled into sarah's childhood bedroom and realized she hadn't left her house since she got home for christmas she claims to have taken an interest in regency era computer games

December 31, 2018 8:32 PM
sarah said we're slowly going to become all the stories we've ever written

December 31, 2018 8:41 PM
sarah says she's going to show me how to bring in the new year chicago style and takes me to a whole foods bar to "pre game"

December 31, 2018 8:55 PM
"look how young i was," sarah says holding her phone up at the whole foods bar to show a picture of her from 2013

December 31, 2018 8:59 PM
"to quote john legend, half of me wants half of you" sarah says after two cans of a beer i've never heard of called 'american'

December 31, 2018 10:03 PM
sarah puts the 'can' in 'american'

December 31, 2018 10:39 PM
drunk sarah took me to her old apartment
building downtown and sang a song in the general
direction of her old room then tried to break in

December 31, 2018 11:34 PM
every time sarah winsd connect 4 she
apologidzes

December 31, 2018 11:39 PM
the way sarah laughyiged then hicuppped
then laufghed again soufnds like the begininfng of
"hungry like the wolf"

December 31, 2018 11:53 PM
the strobe night make me feel like sarah's
back from the bathroom but she's not it's just the
strobe lightsw

january

January 1, 2019 9:15 AM
all sober mornings are the same
all hungover mornings are hungover in their
own way

January 1, 2019 10:09 AM
showed sarah a video i took of her last night
singing to her old apartment and sarah shuddered
and said "who knew so much of my own joy could
bring me so much sadness"
then asked me to replay it

January 1, 2019 11:13 AM
told sarah bosco drunkenly texted me last
night he said he loved me and i didn't know what
to make of it

January 1, 2019 11:38 AM
sarah said google probably knows who we're
in love with even if we don't

January 2, 2019 10:47 AM
being in chicago is not that different from being
in new york we barely ever leave the house

January 2, 2019 12:29 PM
sarah's dad told us asylum seekers are no longer allowed the credible fear interview that could lead to asylum

January 2, 2019 12:32 PM
"credible fear" as a concept

January 2, 2019 3:24 PM
it started snowing again and sarah said if we hide under the blankets the cold might not see us

January 3, 2019 10:49 AM
sarah keeps talking about her cat but when i bring up my childhood dog she loses interest
i don't want to hear about your cat if you don't want to hear about my dog stories it's like oral sex you should reciprocate

January 3, 2019 12:09 PM
sometimes i can't tell if i'm being vain or completely dissociative

January 3, 2019 4:14 PM
sarah is upset i keep winning at bananagrams she said what if the mfa program was just one long game of bananagrams

January 4, 2019 12:24 PM
sarah is having an argument with her dad about U2

January 4, 2019 2:43 PM
haven't had a drink in four days

January 5, 2019 10:01 AM
all hungover mornings are the same
all sober mornings are sober in their own way

January 5, 2019 11:20 AM
sarah is having an argument with her dad
about van morrisson this is maybe just about as
irish as it is ever going to get for me

January 5, 2019 11:43 AM
we are all on the verge of a nervous breakdown

January 6, 2019 11:50 AM
sarah's mom took us out to a client's cabin
for an interior design consultation
the guy said he built the place from scratch
with his two hands and it looked just like the cabin
from the b horror movie i watched with bosco and
elliot

January 6, 2019 12:42 PM
i took a picture of the cabin and sent it to bosco
and sarah remarked "at least you have someone to
send pictures to"

January 6, 2019 8:59 PM
bosco said he's counting down the days till i
get back

January 6, 2019 10:12 PM
i think i miss new york

January 7, 2019 9:13 AM
got a notification reminding me to wish j.j. on his birthday

January 7, 2019 8:20 PM
went to a bar where they let you smoke indoors i drank two gin and tonics and asked sarah if she thinks j.j. has someone to celebrate his birthday with

January 7, 2019 9:45 PM
story idea: a man with gnarly facial hair who spends all holidays alone

January 8, 2019 11:09 AM
haven't spoken to my parents in months and sarah is having an argument with her parents downstairs and i don't want to bog bosco down with my bullshit
i need to deal with my own shit and stop leaning on other people for support

January 8, 2019 12:02 PM
my body is the only thing holding me together

January 8, 2019 4:06 PM
sarah has gossipy hands

January 8, 2019 9:36 PM
sarah is taking me to scarlet bar for disney drag night

January 8, 2019 9:41 PM
we almost missed the train because we were

consulting a reflective surface to reapply our
lipstick it's a little funny

January 9, 2019 10:52 PM
club mixes are like fuckbois i just want them
to commit to like one thing

January 9, 2019 11:01 PM
the girls dancing on the bar table look like
they're learning how to swim (paddle, paddle,
ring-a-don't-a-don't-dong)

January 9 2019 11:28 PM
i would totally fuck a gallagher brother ironi-
cally

January 9, 2019 11:31 PM
camel crush crush crush by paramore

January 9, 2019 11:37 PM
someone at the bar bought us drinks and tried
to flirt with us by telling us he went to princeton
sarah told him she also went to princeton

January 9, 2019 11:46 PM
asked sarah why she lied and she said
"well i have technically been to princeton, new
jersey"

January 9, 2019 11:51 PM
they're playing "the start of something new"
from high school musical and sarah remembers
all the words

January 10, 2019 12:09 AM
all it takes to be a celebrity is to be on disney
channel and then be in rehab for the rest of your life

January 10, 2019 12:13 AM
story idea: a straight white male who goes
into gay clubs to pick up chicks

January 10, 2019 9:14 AM
i woke up with clenched fists today and
instead of analyzing what that meant i was just
like what if a character woke up with clenched fists
what could that mean

January 10, 2019 9:16 AM
favorite new dissociative technique is treating
my own problems as character details

January 11, 2019 11:51 AM
before sarah dropped me off to the airport she
said she thought she would make a good mob wife

January 11, 2019 12:03 PM
bosco wished me a safe flight and said he'd
be waiting for me outside my apartment i think he
definitely "likes me" likes me now

January 12, 2019 11:05 AM
is lana del rey depressed or just recycling
emily dickinson's sadness

January 12, 2019 11:07 AM
am i depressed or just recycling lana del rey's
sadness

January 12, 2019 10:34 PM
bosco told me he was in love with me but not before drinking an entire bottle of wine does it still count

January 13, 2019 10:14 AM
i still try holding on to silly things like nokia placements in pop punk music videos from 2009

January 14, 2019 11:32 PM
i mentioned "beth" by kiss and oscar said that's just peter criss and i felt disproportionately moved by his knowing that and so i kissed him as if to say hey maybe you're like of my kind but i don't know if he got that

January 15, 2019 3:21 PM
told bosco i was going to video chat my little cousin to wish her happy birthday and would he like to say hi and he stayed mostly silent and awkward and forgot to wish her happy birthday

January 15, 2019 3:25 PM
i'm pretty sure they weren't crazy about him

January 16, 2019 11:02 AM
the invention of the ship is also invention of the shipwreck

January 17, 2019 5:24 PM
me: i was birthed prepared
sarah: you're not ever wearing matching socks right now let's calm down

January 18, 2019 11:03 AM
remember being fifteen? i had a flip phone and i think i was genuinely happy

January 18, 2019 9:09 PM
bosco was practicing his portuguese at me and i told him i knew 'sol' meant sun because when i was nine my dad had an affair with a portuguese woman named sol who carved his name into the rio sand and my mom showed me pictures so i could redistribute my animosity between both parents anyway the point of this story is that "rio" by duran duran is a bit of a trigger for me but i'll still sing along sometimes

January 19, 2019 3:29 PM
i aspire to be the girl in the music video with a shirt on in the bathtub

January 20, 2019 10:19 AM
buy toilet paper

January 22, 2019 4:12 PM
natty waved his smoking hand at me and said "look i'm probably not going to get cancer but if i do it's fine i'm motivated by deadlines"

January 23, 2019 8:43 PM
am i good person if my favorite somerset maugham book is the painted veil and i feel like roxy hart at the end of chicago, all alone after having almost everything

January 23, 2019 9:27 PM
scared of being alone but also around most people i just want to leave

January 24, 2019 4:50 PM
remember dating a boy who tried to imitate nabokov but instead of "i tore apart the fantasies of poe and dealt with childhood memories of strange nacreous gleams" you got "call me don quixote. i know you're not up there, cervantes" and it was just like that time you dated a white rapper freshman year of college and he tried to pass off the riff of elton john's "rocket man" as his own

January 25, 2019 8:03 AM
woke up in queens the sun coming in through bosco's curtainless window

January 25, 2019 8:05 AM
what do men in their twenties have against curtains

January 25 2019 8:40 AM
i can hear bosco's upstairs neighbor getting ready for work it seems like the whole world is awake but bosco for whom nine hours of sleep is just not enough

January 25, 2019 8:43 PM
story idea: a writer with writer's block who can't seem to finish a short story and ends up writing about his upstairs neighbor
he's never met her in real life but describes

her through her sounds, the clack clack clack of
sensible shoes at 8:40 in the morning

January 26, 2019 9:03 AM
email julie to tell her your scholarship evaporated

January 28, 2019 9:14 PM
bosco was practicing his portuguese at me
again and when i asked him to translate what he
said he told me it meant "my mother is the most
important woman to me in this world"

January 28, 2019 9:26 PM
thoreau's mom did his laundry during the two
years he camped on ralph waldo emerson's property
at walden pond

January 29, 2019 10:26 PM
lines from "bananafish" i wish exactly applied
to me:
"she was a girl who for a ringing phone
dropped exactly nothing"
"she looked as if her phone had been ringing
continually ever since she had reached puberty"

January 30, 2019 10:09 AM
buy toilet paper

January 30, 2019 8:10 PM
charles kinbote hates women and meat
equally

January 30, 2019 8:13 PM
why are so many hysterical males vegetarian

January 30, 2019 10:13 PM
bosco asked me why sarah has keys to my apartment but he doesn't

february

February 1, 2019 10:55 AM
salena asked me if i'd like to go to victoria's secret with her to buy lingerie and i was like hello i buy penguin underwear in bulk from costco

February 1, 2019 12:34 PM
pedro paramo, juan rulfo

February 1, 2019 1:16 PM
gave bosco keys to my apartment and he hugged me and i swear i saw a tear fall down his face

February 1, 2019 2:39 PM
bosco wrote a story about his upstairs neighbor he compared the sound of her shoes to his mother's

February 1, 2019 2:43 PM
don't know if i'm writing the future or just denying the present

February 1, 2019 11:30 PM
character detail: someone who gets into twitter fights with jenny mccarthy, culture guru

February 1, 2019 11:47 PM
natty and sarah and elliot came over with cheap bourbon and for some reason we started talking about family
natty said strangers are fine but people who love and don't like you are the worst

February 2 ,2019 12:05 AM
i'm just your typical gemini so sad so much

February 2 2019 11.59 AM
woke up to a new group chat about a road trip to dc apparently i invited all my friends to visit my aunt and uncle this weekend?
i have no memory of this

February 2 2019 2.02 PM
story idea: woman who gets fat and stays fat for her job as a plus size social media influencer

February 2 2019 10.22 PM
bosco is upset with me he said i shouldn't have invited natty and sarah and elliot without consulting him first i am not sure what to make of this i thought we were all friends

February 3 2019 11.05 AM
i woke up in a rat's tangle with bosco remembering he held my hand up the stairs and i saw two red pills next to a full glass of water

on the nightstand and i woke up happy because
someone finally loved me as much as sarah
loves chicago and when he woke the first thing
to escape his mouth was "i really miss queens"
and i wished for someone to love me as much as
bosco loves queens

February 3 2019 11.42 AM
he said that it wasn't too much of me it was
too less of him and suddenly i felt like a small and
shrunken thing

February 3 2019 11.58 AM
i was trying to solve boys by listening to the
cure but all the while i had been drowning the boy
i love deep inside of me

February 3, 2019 1:05 PM
why is it that the peel session is almost
always better than the single version

February 4, 2019 2:09 AM
"cool" by gwen stefani is the best break up
song ever written it is also a lie

February 4, 2019 11:39 AM
when bosco tells me he loves me in the
morning it feels like he's a flight attendant miming
with his props as a clinical recording plays in the
background

February 6, 2019 12:24 PM
i think i love new york so much because it
makes me feel famous in a dumb and illusory way

February 7, 2019 10:53 PM
we went to queens and bosco's friends from college came over and one of them invited me to her birthday party she said it was karaoke and heard that i love karaoke and i told her i'll be there

February 7, 2019 11:20 PM
bosco said his friends really like me and he wants me to come with him to the birthday karaoke party and i hugged him it was sweet

February 8, 2019 4:04 PM
sarah booked us a zipcar for the trip to dc this weekend and natty volunteered me as dj which was the first thing that got me excited about this trip

February 8, 2019 6:30 PM
sarah texted me to see if i wanted to hang out and i told her i was going to bosco's friend's birthday party
natty texted me to see if i wanted to hang out and i told him i was going to bosco's friend's birthday party
elliot texted me to see if i wanted to hang out and i told him i was going to bosco's friend's birthday party

February 8, 2019 7:21 PM
was carrying birthday flowers and a six pack so i spent fourteen dollars on an uber pool to k-town but it's fine there'll be karaoke it'll be worth it?

February 8, 2019 7:24 PM
sarah messaged me saying she found salena and elliot at the bar and salena said she suspected that elliot has a crush on someone
i wondered if there was a chance possibly that maybe it was me hypothetically

February 8, 2019 9:26 PM
sarah said that salena told her elliot probably has a crush on her because he said his celebrity crush was zoey deschanel and sarah is also a brunette

February 8, 2019 10:41 PM
drank champagne at karaoke but i still miss my friends

February 9, 2019 2:09 AM
boys they behave like they're fourteen years old they pick a fight with you at karaoke and then they pick a fight with you on the train and then they ask you not to wheel your emotional baggage into a new relationship and then they stop at a key foods in queens to pick up a snack for their roommate in the middle of the fight and when you grab a bag of kettle chips because you forgot about dinner they don't even offer to pay for it even though they are already ahead of you in line and then outside their building they cry and then they say you made them cry and then they yell at you about the invalidity of their feelings

February 9, 2019 2:22 AM
told bosco he doesn't need to go with us on the road trip tomorrow but he told me to go to sleep because i'm not thinking straight i think i'm thinking straighter than i ever was in fact my anger has sobered me

February 9, 2019 2:31 AM
bosco broke down in tears how is that i'm the one consoling him

February 9, 2019 3:33 AM
remembered that i left my old record player in my aunt's basement at least there's one thing to look forward to on this trip

February 9, 2019 8:11 AM
we're on the train back to manhattan to get our stuff together for the trip and bosco still hasn't said a single word to me is this what the whole trip is going to be like

February 9, 2019 9:03 AM
sarah pulls up in front of my apartment we haven't even put our bags in the trunk yet and the first thing she says is that she's thinking about changing her number to a 773 because she misses chicago

February 9, 2019 9:07 AM
asked sarah where's elliot and she said they all hung out last night and he said he wasn't going to make it he had a lot of work to do and i felt sad

February 9, 2019 9:38 AM

we pick up natty and he calls shotgun they seem to be having so much fun upfront meanwhile bosco has been asleep since pretty much as soon as he got in

February 9, 2019 10:16 AM

natty hands me the phone to dj and i declare we exclusively play new jersey artists on the turnpike springsteen jonas brothers and my chemical romance

February 9, 2019 10:20 AM

natty said you can't play chicken driving in new jersey because everyone wants to die more than you

February 9, 2019 11:18 AM

natty and i smoked a cigarette at the rest stop and he asked me what's wrong i told him that bosco picked a fight with me at karaoke because i patted his shoulder extra hard when a smiths song came on and he accused me of invalidating his feelings and didn't pay for my bag of kettle chips

natty handed me another cigarette from his pack

February 9, 2019 11:23 AM

sarah said she misses 2007, when burger king still had battered fries

February 9, 2019 12:45 PM

natty had to take a call so we stopped at another rest stop this one was named after walt whitman sarah looked at me sighed and said "we exist as we are and that is enough"

i hope she's wrong

February 9, 2019 1:13 PM
the car isn't starting the battery is dead and bosco is still asleep

February 9, 2019 2:02 PM
all happy zip cars are alike all unhappy zip cars break down in new jersey

February 9, 2019 2:02 PM
elliot texted me a picture of sarah's cat he said that after he feeds her he reads bellow to her because she's a chicago cat and everybody knows all chicago cats like bellow

February 10, 2019 1:05 AM
finally get to my aunt's and i asked bosco if he wanted to step out with me for a smoke and he said why don't you just step out with natty it's snowing outside and it's cold and i told him he was missing the point and when he finally stepped outside he complained about me blowing smoke in his face and then i told him to go back inside and then the snow melted into rain and he put my hood up because i had been sick the past week and he didn't want me to get sick again and i thought that was sweet but i also wondered if it made sense for a person like me to be in a relationship with someone who not only loved but genuinely liked their mother so much

February 10, 2019 11:38 AM
at the hirschorn and sarah looks at a paul klee painting and turns to me and says "my grandmother made a quilt like this once"

February 10, 2019 11:38 AM
told sarah i like reginald marsh's depression
era because i'm also depressed and in new york

February 10, 2019 4:05 PM
natty said he was lighting a cigarette outside
the beer garden and some guy came up to tried to
buy the broken bic lighter off of him

February 10, 2019 9:35 PM
instead of pandering to my aunt i find that i'm
always trying to ensure that bosco is comfortable

February 10, 2019 10:31 PM
my aunt drank lots of wine and took me aside
in the kitchen and said she really likes natty and
sarah
that felt pointed

February 11, 2019 9:02 AM
bosco carried my old record player from the
basement and brought it to the car this is the
nicest thing he's done for me all week

February 11, 2019 11:05 AM
on the drive back to new york bosco lent me
his copy of lispector's "passion according to g.h." in
which he underlined "i'm afraid to begin composing
in order to be understood by the imaginary someone" and i felt like i was intruding

February 13, 2019 6:30 PM
i was looking up a song on bosco's phone

and rilo kiley appeared in his recent searches and i looked at him and he said what! i didn't wanna make a big deal out of listening to the music you like! it was nice

February 13, 2019 8:26 PM
hanging out with bosco feels like the tail end of a cigarette it gets better before it's almost over

February 13, 2019 9:02 PM
got bosco and sarah tickets to see a smiths cover band on valentine's day i'm very excited i bet sarah a drink they'd play "sheila take a bow"

February 14, 2019 10:07 AM
don't ever want to be friends with anyone who makes a valentine's day post again

February 14, 2019 11:23 AM
buy toilet paper and trash bags

February 14, 2019 4:07 PM
professor told me bad relationships are always a good start to any kind of art maybe he's right

February 14, 2019 10:54 PM
they played "sheila take a bow" and boy did that drink taste good

February 14, 2019 11:47 PM
growing up is realizing you can be beloved without being loved

February 15, 2019 12:02 AM
i had no intention of going out on a fancy date but i kept waiting for bosco to acknowledge that it's valentine's day

February 15, 2019 2:18 PM
as i get older i find that i startle more easily

February 16, 2019 6:30 PM
i feel more anxious about sleeping alone than about not sleeping together

February 16, 2019 7:49 PM
a) you don't have to go home but you can't stay here
b) you don't have to stay here but you can go home
c) you don't have to go home and you can stay here
d) you don't have to go home and you can like totally stay here

February 16, 2019 11:41 PM
in all the time paul and linda were together they only spent eleven nights apart

February 17, 2019 1:07 AM
maybe i don't want to be alone because i'm afraid of finding out i'm still sad that i might never stop being sad

February 17, 2019 2:57 AM
the a/c switched to energy saver mode and the

room is searing again and i miss the stodgy sound
that made me feel full and safe and less alone

February 18, 2019 9:04 AM
there are pictures of brown women with red
lipstick smoking cigarettes on bosco's bedroom
wall

February 19, 2019 10:39 AM
woke up from a dream and told bosco in it i
had slick short hair and wore these ultracool denim
overalls the kind with straps you could tie around
the shoulder and i told him i was sad because i
looked so cool in the dream and it's over and he
told me i always look cool and he looked soft and
sincere and i believed that he believes that he loves
me

February 19, 2019 11:01 PM
elliot and sarah and natty came over and
we played cards because sometimes we need
the supernatural force of a laminated bicycle
deck to tell us when to start pouring

February 19, 2019 11:39 PM
we were smoking on the fire escape and
saw the neighbors across the street fucking and i
thought about the woman j.j. used to watch from
his fire escape

February 19, 2019 11:42 PM
i remember at first thinking j.j. was being tender
with his observations because he pointed at her
display of empty wine bottles by the window and said

women have a way of turning their problems into something beautiful but then he started describing the shape of her body in the shower and the way she undressed and made coffee in the morning without putting pants on

February 20, 2019 12:05 AM
sarah said she loves touching her eyes because it makes her feel like a lizard

February 20, 2019 12:09 AM
sarah said she joined an ivy league dating app called "the league"

February 20, 2019 12:22 AM
natty said "find me on the league" is the new "meet me in montauk"

February 20, 2019 12:36 AM
story idea: sarah reports everyone who likes her on the league

February 20, 2019 3:36 AM
dreamt a girl used to let a guy pee in her mouth because he claimed when he was younger and in boarding school he would imagine sex to feel like the sensation of peeing

February 20, 2019 10:12 AM
i may never be the kind of person who listens to a podcast over a boyband

February 21, 2019 4:01 PM
sat in class for an hour listening to people

describe the thinly veiled character that is me they said "she" was witty and reflective and self-destructive and charming and had daddy issues

February 21, 2019 4:23 PM
asked natty if he thought i was self-destructive he said no then paused and added "well you're not on any hard drugs"

February 21, 2019 11:18 PM
bosco keeps stressing that it's my friend group but i thought we shared our friends guess this means i get to keep them in the event of a discourse

February 21, 2019 1:28 AM
guy at bar told me that the da vinci code was both his favorite book and movie

February 22, 2019 2:09 AM
natty asked me what it is with me and white rappers and then told me he thinks that jason derulo might be a bad boyfriend

February 22, 2019 2:24 AM
"toto" by africa plays at the bar and elliot and natty get into a fight about hemingway because the kilimanjaro doesn't rise from the serengeti

February 22, 2019 11:04 AM
my friends and i might be potential alcoholics but we really put the 'fun' in functioning

February 23, 2019 5:27 PM
elliot asked me where bosco was because he hadn't seen him lately and i didn't know how to tell him bosco blew me off to spend the day toasting frosted mugs and salt rimmed cocktails with salena in brooklyn

February 23, 2019 5:33 PM
growing tired of answering my friends when they ask me why he's never here

February 23, 2019 9:27 PM
sarah is describing the smell of chicago to krista

February 24, 2019 1:50 AM
~~hey bosco i know you once said you don't want to invalidate your own feelings and i get that and i also don't want to invalidate mine but you went out for dinner with another girl and she picked up the tab and it hurt me and i haven't seen you since thursday and i don't even know where you are or when you're going home and i don't wanna be in this if it makes me feel as lonely as i was before i don't want to be in this if i'm going to be spending the night crying on sarah's stoop having both sides of the conversation in my head and it hurts because when we fought on the train i told you i had baggage and you said let's not bring baggage into this but you know where i'm coming from you were here for a lot of it and you know all about me and still you can't figure out what i want or what i need and if we were still just friends i would have texted you about how~~

~~this boy treated me tonight and you would've~~
~~dropped everything and taken the train to me~~
~~i don't get it we sang along to the beach boys~~
~~together you should know you shouldn't go steady~~
~~if you're not ready because it wouldn't be right to~~
~~leave your best girl home on a saturday night~~

February 24, 2019 10:10 AM
woke up on sarah's couch to coffee and
toast i think she feels bad for me i'm literally right
back where i was two months ago and it's all too
familiar

February 24, 2019 2:28 PM
sarah asked me if i ever heard back from
bosco and i shook my head no and she said let's
treat ourselves and plugged in the gone girl dvd
and played the director's cut

February 24, 2019 3:40 PM
bosco finally texted me and said his phone had
died and he slept in and he is on his way to me
i asked sarah if she has any whiskey on hand

February 24, 2019 5:40 PM
bosco showed up at my doorstep bearing
gifts in a rough trade store bag i think because he
grew up with no money he expects a forty dollar
double LP to buy my forgiveness

February 25, 2019 1:27 AM
bosco said it was really hard for him he grew
up in a trailer and finds it hard to turn down an all
expenses paid lunch date with salena he said i

wouldn't know what it's like to have a childhood
that hard

February 25, 2019 2:03 AM
        i remember the roof of changi airport felt
open and bruised like the surface current of a city
underwater and my parents took me to the butterfly
garden and then the sunflower garden and then
the orchid garden and then we gave up smiling and
sat at the terminal 3 starbucks with our luggage
cart loaded with laminated shopping bags from the
cocoa tree that swarmed with novelty american
chocolate one of my parents bought to appease the
other and my dad handed me a tall hot chocolate
and a cherry lollipop wrapped in polka-dotted craft
paper twirling down its stem and congratulated me
for making it out of the country for the first time and
i thought about the casio sa-76 portable keyboard i
left behind at my grandparents' home in new delhi
and remember my mom telling me i should thank
her brother in law for the gift and i remember her
asking her brother in law how she looked in the
turquoise dress she got tailored after i got out of
the hospital from my appendicitis surgery and i
remember the anger on her face when i looked over
her shoulder at the internet café and she gave me
shit for not respecting her privacy and i remember
talking to my dad on the phone he told me he'd be
flying in the next day and i remember on the drive
back from the airport he told me he wished for
the plane to crash and i remember the first thing i
thought when dad told me she'd been fucking my
uncle all along i thought it meant she was abandon-
ing me to mother my cousin

i was seven
sarah once told me children don't learn to
empathize till they're eight

February 25, 2019 3:39 AM
when we moved to indonesia i was so
psyched to not be living in a small apartment for
the first time we had a mango tree in the front yard
and i mean we had a front yard and the mangos
always fell from the tree prematurely and it makes
sense that i never really grew to like the taste
of ripe mangos and i remember when we found
a snake in the drain pipes and i remember the
guards across the street next to the donut kiosk
the sprinkles were pink they were always pink
and i'd never had a donut before and i remember
the guards they would play chess late into the
night and they would try to speak in english with
me and i tried to describe to them a plastic bag
this one time and i kept saying "poly-thene" and
gesturing in vain with my hands and when they
finally got what i was trying to say they said "oh
iya itu namanya plastik" and then the novelty of a
new place and the novelty of the new food wore
off and the one fish place that we'd always go to
felt gross like being underwater like being in a fish
tank and the fights got louder and i started noticing
the lizards that snaked and wagged electrically all
around the house and i grew tired of watching the
same dubbed version of prisoner of azkaban that
always aired at three pm on cable and i missed
speaking a language i wholly understood

February 25, 2019 3:50 AM
when bosco said i couldn't imagine what
a difficult childhood was like i sat still and said
nothing

march

March 1, 2019 11:39 AM
dreamt i kept breaking out into hives and my
neck grew red and blotchy

March 2, 2019 2:35 AM
i wanna be like lana del rey sexy sad and
satirical

March 3, 2019 1:29 PM
natty's birthday is coming up and sarah has
been sending me links to different whiskey stones
she is considering

March 4, 2019 5:12 PM
inflate leftover balloons
happy birthday banner (duane reade) party hats
vegan pizza
vegan pasta

March 5, 2019 12:51 PM
why do the saddest songs have the most
hand claps

March 5, 2019 2:33 PM
if sarah sends me another link to an online whiskey merchandise i will tell her to maybe consider getting natty a matching set for his fiancée

March 5, 2019 2:35 PM
everybody always forgets about the fiancée cake?

March 7, 2019 10:43 PM
bosco drinks a bottle of wine and tells me he loves me he tells me he's so happy i picked him when i had options
i told him he never took me out on a date

March 7, 2019 11:43 PM
sarah followed me into the kitchen to bring out the cake and told me she might be in love with natty
there were many things i'd have liked to say to her but i didn't know how

March 8, 2019 10:41 AM
sarah calls me from the ten a.m. greyhound going anywhere she says she misses me but i know she's calling me because she misses natty

March 8, 2019 10:49 AM
sarah calls me all the time when she's alone and i inherently understand that but

March 9, 2019 2:24 PM
buy toilet paper

March 10, 2019 10:26 PM
natty and i are doing movie night at sarah's because sarah is out of town

March 11, 2019 1:32 AM
natty is doing sarah's dishes he keeps trying to scrub the fake printed coffee stains off of the luke's coffee cups

March 11, 2019 9:46 AM
story idea: girl wakes up in her friend's apartment where she is catsitting and listens to the radio station instead of doing work and the voice on the radio says it's amphibian and reptile weather it's march and frogs will crop up on the highway like magnolia and then she goes on to discogs and spends twenty minutes studying beach boys christmas tapes

March 11, 2019 11:22 AM
natty and i drank coffee and listened to lana and we decided to get bagels in pajamas despite the rain because we thought it'd be cute and fun and on the way there he asked me if it was obvious he was in love with sarah and i told him to call things off with his fiancée maybe

March 11, 2019 8:19 PM
train wasn't running so i took an uber pool to meet bosco at the angelika and as we drove past bryant park i remembered brendon asked me to meet him here one fall we got coffee at that starbucks

March 11, 2019 8:21 PM
one city, ten thousand landmarks of romantic misdemeanor

March 11, 2019 8:59 PM
told bosco natty and sarah have feelings for each other he said he thinks it's all a bad idea they're not in love with each other they're just used to being around each other

March 11, 2019 10:12 PM
i let myself get all excited about gloria bell because it was our first real date and i read that tyson ritter from the all american rejects plays the raging upstairs neighbor in it but bosco spent the movie whispering parallels between julianne moore's character and his mother he said they're both free spirited and they both like dancing

March 11, 2019 10:19 PM
how didn't he see me in gloria bell clearly i'm the one falling into bed with disappointing men

March 11, 2019 11:12 PM
the trains still weren't running regularly so bosco and i waited a half hour at the thirty fourth street station at herald square watching tourists wave their hands in front of the horizontal green bars to activate the christopher janney audio installation and when we finally got home bosco pointed out how the walk to my apartment from the train station feels a lot longer than the walk from the station to his apartment in queens even though it's not

i wanted to ask him to leave to give me back my keys i wanted to say if this doesn't feel like home maybe stop getting your mail delivered here and go back home to queens instead but i was too hungry and tired to fight so i made us dinner instead

March 12 2019 10:30 PM
julianne moore's boobs get a lot of screen time in gloria bell

March 12, 2019 11:54 AM
natty said this program would be great if it weren't for the fucking writers

March 12, 2019 11:56 AM
story idea: a fucking writer who fucking writes

March 13, 2019 11:05 PM
when i say something dumb bosco crushes my shoulders and compresses my face like slime like playdough and he tells me he just wants to squinch me and i ask him if squinch is portmanteau for squeeze and pinch and he squinches me and says it's just what it is it's squinch and i let him

March 13, 2019 11:35 PM
bosco squints his right eye when he's being sincere

March 13, 2019 11:37 PM
bosco only calls me baby when he's inside me

March 14, 2019 11:15 PM
told natty i have a hard time falling asleep

without a record on he told me when he got back to his apartment after a string of nights spent on sarah's couch it was dark and he switched the lamp on and it was the first time in a while he'd been there long enough to turn that lamp on

March 15, 2019 8:21 AM
fell asleep on the wrong 7 train and woke up deep in queens by a construction worker who grabbed my ass and offered me weed

March 15, 2019 12:01 PM
woke up hungover and with a sharp pain in my legs so decided to walk thirty blocks to the record store to show my body who's in control

March 15, 2019 2:35 PM
told bosco my legs hurt and i'm probably not in the best condition to commute to queens but he said he'd roll me a j when we get to queens

March 16, 2019 3:54 PM
i was in the e.r. and sarah rented a car and picked me up from bosco's and bosco never got in the car he just went back to bed and natty cut class and sarah pushed her flight back to take care of me and elliot came and he brought vegan ice cream and bosco still didn't show

March 16, 2019 3:56 PM
we went to sarah's after i got discharged and we watched the gilmore girls episode where they devil egg jess's car

March 16, 2019 3:58 PM
the worst part about dating men in new york city is that you can't devil egg their car because they don't have one

March 16, 2019 4:01 PM
can't even play mind games with bosco because he's just that impervious

March 16, 2019 4:15 PM
natty said bosco dresses like a boy but wants to be treated like a man

March 16, 2019 11:15 PM
bosco showed up five hours too late he held me and cried and told me he was scared of disappointing me he said he said he thought one day i'd grow tired of being disappointed and leave him
i told him i wasn't going to leave him

March 17, 2019 9:30 AM
bosco said he wanted to take me back to my apartment because sarah might be "misery-ing" me

March 17, 2019 10:15 AM
bosco asked me if he should cancel movie night with his roommates to take care of me since i was still limping

March 18, 2019 8:34 AM
the people i knew back when starbucks still gave out free songs where did they go what happened to them

March 18, 2019 9:19 PM
bosco got me more weed for the pain and
we got high and listened to a flock of seagulls
he asked me if i thought the guy from a flock of
seagulls does that thing to his hair to look like a
seagull

March 18, 2019 9:21 PM
why do all flock of seagulls albums look like
they could be covers for documentaries about
aliens

March 18, 2019 9:22 PM
sleeveless in seattle

March 19, 2019 8:42 PM
bosco said he wanted to volunteer at a
publishing event and asked if i would be ok
getting by without him for a night and i tried my
best not to laugh

March 19, 2019 8:57 PM
sarah and natty and elliot came over and sarah
takes two hits off a j and swings back and forth on
my desk chair and says it's swinging too fast it must
be broken

March 19, 2019 8:59 PM
not even nine pm and elliot points out for the
second time how "nine in the afternoon" by panic
at the disco makes no sense

March 19, 2019 10:29 PM

elliot is trying to solve tracy chapman's "fast car" like a word problem he is tallying the total number of people who got in her car

March 19, 2019 10:31 PM

elliot is having an argument about key lime pie he is in a corner getting angry because key lime pie isn't "really pie" key lime pie is cake

March 19, 2019 10:35 PM

natty asked elliot if he thinks french silk pie is cake elliot said yes

March 19, 2019 10:45 PM

german chocolate cake is pie boston cream is cake cheesecake is pie
birthday cake is pie
lemon chess is pie
kentucky derby pie is cake
chicago deep dish is cake
the city of chicago is cake
apple pie is cake
new york cheesecake is pie
natty's new sunglasses are pie
ratio of a circle's circumference to its diameter is cake new york pizza pie is pie
cake the band is pie
lasagna is pie
pie is pie
cake is pie

March 19, 2019 10:51 PM

time is a flat pie

112

March 19, 2019 10:57 PM
pumpkin pie is cake
mooncake is cake
peach pie is cake

March 19, 2019 10:59 PM
time is a piece of wax dripping on a pie

March 19, 2019 11:23 PM
mint juul is cake
mango juul is pie
we are all cake
everything that is cake is pie
everything that never was isn't cake
avril lavigne's replacement body double is pie
pie is cake
layer cake (film) is pie

March 19, 2019 11:29 PM
elliot reminds me of jon from garfield

March 19, 2019 11:32 PM
elliot caught me looking at him and asked me
to show him what i was typing on my notes app
and then his face turned red i don't think he liked
being compared to jon from garfield

March 19, 2019 11:45 PM
stoned sarah led me into the kitchen because
she wanted to tell me something in confidence she
got all dramatic and told me i can't tell anyone and
then i said what! and she told me elliot had feelings
for me and he'd met up with natty at a sports bar to
talk about them

March 19, 2019 11:57 PM
elliot has feelings for me and I just compared him to jon from garfield

March 20, 2019 2:03 AM
elliot said he felt bad for leaving me alone while i was sick i told him i was fine and he said no you're not you're limping from one corner of the bedroom to another

March 20 2019 3:19 AM
bosco came home drunk and said he took a cab back from brooklyn because he wanted to get back to me as soon as possible because he couldn't bear being away from me he went in for a hug but threw up all over my sheets instead

March 20, 2019 4:14 PM
bosco told me he wants to be in a vacuum with his spanish

March 21, 2019 10:03 AM
sarah came over to take me to the rheumatol-ogist and it was the first time i'd left the apartment in a week
i forgot there was a weather outside

March 21, 2019 2:13 PM
the rheumatologist looked at the tests and said there is something wrong with me but she couldn't quite put her finger on what just yet
specialists are just people you spend a $30 co-pay on to tell you something you already knew

March 21, 2019 4:32 PM

told sarah at least we have a new jenny lewis record to look forward to tomorrow

March 21, 2019 4:46 PM

natty drove to pittsburgh to break up with his fiancée sarah says she's not anxious but she keeps checking her horoscope

March 21, 2019 4:48 PM

jenny lewis says mercury hasn't been in retrograde for that long

March 22, 2019 5:07 PM

i wish my sadness and solitude were as cool as jenny lewis's sadness and solitude

March 22, 2019 5:56 PM

bosco texted me to tell me he loves me and he loves jenny lewis but won't be able to come over for the listening party because he just wants to hang with his friends for a change

March 22, 2019 7:15 PM

this listening party is now just me playing music videos on the projector and sarah checking her horoscope

March 22, 2019 7:54 PM

told sarah it's been a while since a conversation we had passed the bechdel test

March 22, 2019 8:20 PM
sarah asked me why i change out of pajamas whenever elliot tells me he's coming over 62

March 22, 2019 9:49 PM
we decided to put karaoke videos on the projector and elliot first sang "tequila" then "margaritaville"
he would

March 23, 2019 1:43 AM
elliot and i were watching final destination when he told me he lost his mom in a plane crash

March 24, 2019 2:25 PM
bosco told me he wrote a sex scene once and zadie smith liked it he said the thing about a sex scene is that it isn't that different from the experience good sex is good for a while and then it gets boring and then it's over

March 25, 2019 3:37 AM
i cook for him i mince the garlic peel the ginger chop the onions dice the peppers press the lime till the juice splashes my face splotches the red seams of my dress i make the sauce from scratch i glide the knife across the cutting board set the vegetables into the pan with two sprigs of thyme i add water from the tap by the spoonful and watch the liquid spume over the open flame i pour it over cored jackfruit flesh on the plate until the fluid slips and slithers and when he lifts the fork to his mouth and back to the plate i wait for him to say something but he doesn't he repeats

the motion without saying a word and when he
finishes he leaves his dish unsoaked

March 26, 2019 6:45 PM
sarah told me she loves me as much as she
loves chicago

March 27, 2019 8:35 PM
someone in workshop asked me how my
character could have undergone so much trauma
without it having transformed her they wanted to
know why "she" wasn't balled up on the couch
after the thing with j.j. and i didn't know what to say
except not all trauma is transformative some of us
like to think of the bad as little as possible

March 28, 2019 4:39 AM
dreamt of rotting fruit

March 28, 2019 1:29 PM
sprained my wrist chopping beets it looks like
there's dried blood on the cutting board

March 28, 2019 3:04 PM
natty told me his friend ben wants to meet
me so he can be in my book

March 28, 2019 6:21 PM
bosco said he hates the smell of my cigarettes

March 29, 2019 6:45 PM
bosco told me he made plans to get dinner and
watch a movie with carly he asked me if that's ok and
i told him dinner and a movie sounds like a date just

like what happened with salena and he said that's
just his way of hanging out with his friends

March 30, 2019 11:21 PM
told sarah i was fantasizing about faking a
gone girl scenario to put bosco to the test she
said she'd help me stage it but nobody has fun
during a fire drill

March 30, 2019 11:37 PM
sarah said she had a fire drill in seventh
grade and during it a bird pooped on her head
and they didn't know what to do so they sent her
to the clinic and let her go home
i told her seventh grade was hard for me too
because joel madden got nicole richie pregnant i
was at the mall with my mother when i found out i
told her i needed a minute

March 31, 2019 1:20 PM
ordered takeout from the chinese place that
always forgets to charge me they said the food is
spicy "no refund order at your own risk"
i asked for extra chili oil

april

April 1 2019 12:40 PM
whenever things get complicated bosco runs away to queens

April 1, 2019 1:48 PM
why does bosco behave like he was the one who was homeschooled

April 2, 2019 2:34 PM
you give things time to heal and self correct like your wrist like your relationship with bosco and you wait and when they don't self correct you take matters into your own broken hands

April 2, 2019 4:23 PM
elliot: asks you if he can keep you company in the waiting room, sends you pictures of dogs to cheer you up when you tell him he doesn't need to worry about it
bosco, person you are dating: amiss, leaves clothes in a tangle on the floor while your wrist is broken, leaves takeout in your room, tells you whenever he is with you that he misses queens

April 3, 2019 6:08 PM

we loaded bosco's shit in the car and drove to queens and i asked natty if i should give him another chance to explain himself and natty queued up the live version of leonard cohen's "first we take manhattan" and sarah pulled the car over and turned on the headlights and handed bosco the ikea bag with his records and books and it felt like we were in a movie

April 3, 2019 7:46 PM

taylor swift said loving jake gyllenhall was like driving a brand new maserati down a dead end street i told sarah and natty loving bosco was like having a zip car break down in the middle of nowhere new jersey leaving us stranded at walt whitman rest stop for five hours while we waited for triple a

April 4, 2019 9:49 PM

overheard at bar: everything we do is psychologically sustainable

April 4, 2019 9:54 PM

guy at bar asked me who my favorite beatle is and offered to buy me a drink

April 4, 2019 10:06 PM

men who like the beatles too much are like men who like their mother too much

April 4, 2019 10:08 PM

told natty my favorite beatle is yoko he said his favorite beatle is mark david chapman

April 5, 2019 7:32 PM
the last song bosco and i listened to together was "i'm gonna run away" by joan jett and the blackhearts

April 5, 2019 8:14 PM
a breakup playlist that begins with "don't think twice it's alright" by bob dylan and ends with "don't think twice it's alright" by dolly parton

April 5, 2019 8:21 PM
natty said it's not a playlist at this point it's an execution

April 6, 2019 7:47 PM
ben told natty he wished bosco was white so he could hate him more

April 6, 2019 7:53 PM
ben also told natty my writing made him feel the way frank ocean makes him feel like he wanted to die but also have sex
i also want to die and have sex not necessarily in that order

April 6, 2019 9:28 PM
haven't had sex in eight days

April 6, 2019 10:45 PM
remember when things were nice remember when we stayed up talking and drinking and fell asleep at four and forgot to eat and woke up an hour later and went out in the snow and all we

could find were hash browns and we ate them with dijon mustard and kissed in the kitchen listening to regina spektor and i was in love both feet off the ground

April 7, 2019 7:53 PM
ryan adams used music to control mandy moore

April 7, 2019 8:58 PM
~~bosco i just wanna fucking call you and talk about the things we have in common you used to get me in so many specific ways you found the brian eno record i really like in the dollar stacks you liked the same mexican beer i liked and you knew that to me fancy meant pouring the beer into mason jars with a slice of lime instead of drinking it straight from the bottle but that doesn't change how you never showed up for me and i'm grieving the loss of my best friend and it hurts and it hurts over and over again that you never showed up at my doorstep or got drunk and sent me a text saying you missed me and you never fought for me or asked me to stay i wanted you i needed to hear you ask me to stay even though it probably would've changed nothing~~

April 8, 2019 7:23 AM
i wanna be like lana i wanna look like my bras fit well under tshirts

April 8, 2019 8:05 AM
after the breakup i make my bed every morning after the breakup i come home to a made bed every night after the breakup i wake up alone

every day and feel just fine
after the breakup i close out the bars
after the breakup i run around with my friends
without feeling guilty
after the breakup i smudge the apartment
with sage
after the breakup i bring a man back to my
room and lie with him in bed awkwardly after the
breakup i feel more angry than sad and then more
sad than angry and then just disappointed
after the breakup i don't text him
after the breakup i do text him
after the breakup i regret texting him because
he disappoints me again
after the breakup i take my vitamins regularly

April 8, 2019 9:15 AM
i've never had a sober first kiss

April 8, 2019 11:01 AM
dreamt i was haunted

April 8, 2019 12:20 PM
story idea: pregnancy as hostage taking

April 8, 2019 11:09 PM
elliot asked if he could kiss me i said yes and
let him

April 9, 2019 7:18 PM
whenever i ask the person i'm going out with
if it'd be ok if i use their name in the book they say
yes of course yes and i think it's cute how they
think they're incapable of being bad

April 10, 2019 8:26 PM
elliot keeps trying to reach for my hand but it's broken like literally

April 11, 2019 10:02 PM
i just wanna take a nap together i don't wanna watch a movie and do it right

April 11, 2019 7:06 AM
told bosco to stop sending me itemized lists of his things every day because my wrist is broken and it physically hurts to carry the things he left behind

April 11, 2019 7:52 AM
staring out the window and it took me minutes to realize it was raining

April 11, 2019 10:14 AM
sarah told me she bought natty and elliot and me tickets to the white sox game and we're all going

April 12, 2019 4:56 PM
story idea: a tender connection between two unhappy people

April 12, 2019 10:48 PM
salt has zero calories

April 13, 2019 7:15 AM
nancy spungen doesn't get enough credit for being the most talented sex pistol

April 13, 2019 7:19 AM
i wasn't the nancy to his id but his mother was definitely the ann beverly to his sid

April 13, 2019 9:12 AM
the concept of love is ominous

April 13, 2019 11:07 AM
we're probably both listening to the same mitski album in different boroughs

April 13, 2019 12:18 PM
after the breakup i apparently go to baseball games

April 13, 2019 2:58 PM
natty said the smile cam is brought to you by frank's red hot not the hot sauce but the s.t.d. only baseball players get

April 13, 2019 3:10 PM
at the game i jokingly cheered for the red sox and the guy seated in front of us jokingly got mad at me and asked me if i wanted to fight i pointed at my splint and said you should look at the other guy then i whispered to elliot i don't even know what the red sox play in fact i don't even own matching sox i had some beer

April 13, 2019 4:41 PM
we sat on a park bench in the bronx after the game and i said i felt american let's play springsteen we poured whiskey into plastic cups i played "stolen car" and elliot played "ain't good enough for you"

April 13, 2019 9:39 PM
keep coming home to more of bosco's mail

April 14, 2019 8:07 PM
~~hey elliot i like you i do but i'm still getting bosco's records delivered to my mailing address and the other day i reached out for the box of ginger snaps in the pantry and i found a singular double stuft oreo left behind from the pack bosco bought and i thought about how he's gone but stupid dumb traces of his presence remain and it feels cheap even though it shouldn't to be moving on and i think i need to not be with him and not be with you and i think i need to be alone i might even want to be alone for the first time in a long time and maybe have meaningless sex with a stranger or not or maybe even just watch duck soup in bed alone with a bag of popcorn chips and let the crumbs fall onto the sheets and not worry about it and maybe you can wait for me or maybe you can't but you certainly don't have to and maybe the truth is that i like you but i just i need a hot second~~

April 14, 2019 9:46 PM
buy:
candles
cigarettes
febreeze
tofu
vodka
seltzer

April 14, 2019 10:59 PM
four signs you're about to die of a heart
attack: a targeted ad

April 14, 2019 11:34 PM
~~i went to the white sox game with sarah and~~
~~natty and elliot yesterday and i walked from my~~
~~apartment to hundred and eighteenth with a can~~
~~of beer in my bag at eleven listening to "your best~~
~~american girl" i walked on morningside ave in-~~
~~stead of amsterdam because i wanted to be near~~
~~a park so i could scream into the sky intermittently~~
~~and without judgement and on the walk there~~
~~there were women wearing all black smoking~~
~~cigarettes in the heat too and i debated opening~~
~~the can of beer to see what would happen maybe~~
~~a cop would stop by and maybe i would get de-~~
~~ported so i could maybe be sad about something~~
~~else for a change i didn't do that instead i smoked~~
~~a cigarette and then another when i saw elliot juul-~~
~~ing on sarah's stoop i walked in circles around her~~
~~block listening to mitski and i wrote down a note~~
~~on my phone about how you and i are probably~~
~~both listening to the same mitski song in different~~
~~boroughs and i opened the can on the way up to~~
~~sarah's apartment and showed up with a smile on~~
~~my face and said to everyone in the room "look~~
~~how sports i am i am wearing all black and also i~~
~~showed up with an open can of bud light i am very~~
~~sports i am so sports" but as i walked in i asked if~~
~~sarah had a spare pair of black sunglasses i could~~
~~borrow because my favorite pair of sunglasses is~~
~~lost and also i wanted to disappear and we went~~

to the game and the white sox lost and i didn't
care and i almost got into a fight and elliot kept
trying to take my hand and i wanted to give it to
him so badly i really did but i couldn't understand
why it felt cheap and awful because he had been
in all the waiting rooms with me when you weren't
there you were never there and when he wasn't
there he sent me pictures of dogs until he showed
up with vegan ice cream and whenever he brings
chips he always makes sure they're vegan and
when we got back home there was a package and
i didn't let elliot take it up for me because i don't
want him to carry my baggage your package your
baggage because you made me feel like my baggage is my own and not to be shared and it killed
me bosco it killed me and i would have let it go i
would've let everything go if you'd have shown up
at my doorstep that wednesday night when everything went to shit but you never came you never
fought for me and i remembered how you told me
you'd never let me go you meant you wanted for
me to stay but you let me leave you didn't fight
you let me go so easy you didn't ask me to stay
you didn't fight for me and the nights come back
to me that night when we stayed up drinking and
forgetting to eat and we woke up at four hungry
and it was snowing and we kissed on the kitchen
tiles and i felt loved and i felt in love and now it's
sunday and i'm listening to your mitski record
and drinking vodka and water because i have
been drinking too much whiskey and coke and it's
starting to show and i want you to know i never
gave you the keys with the intent of taking them
away and it hurt to drop your shit off in queens

~~in that fucking ikea bag and i never thought we'd be merging our records together only to separate them months later and i can only imagine you felt the same way but i won't ever know for sure because you never had a conversation with me you just let me talk at you and said i'm sorry and i just want you remember when you told me you always feel relieved when someone abandons you because you always feel like everyone's going to abandon you and when it happens you feel relieved and i should've known and now here i am drinking vodka listening to mitski writing you this letter and even though i ended it i am the one who feels abandoned i just want you to know no one's ever disappointed me like you~~

April 14, 2019 11:58 PM
my mom did a really good job of making me feel small by calling me big

April 15, 2019 5:57 PM
haven't masturbated since i was thirteen

April 15, 2019 8:28 PM
didn't think the songs i sang in the kitchen making coffee that tuesday morning would have gained significance but here i am listening to lana servin' up god in a burnt coffee pot

April 16, 2019 7:49 AM
dreamt he kept posting pictures of ramones records i wanted on his instastory

132

April 16, 2019 5:16 PM
renata adler twitter bot called speedbot

April 16, 2019 8:44 PM
sarah said the sawing of skull at cadaver
camp smelled like cheetos sarah said she misses
cleaning tendons

April 16, 2019 9:54 PM
i want my apartment to look and feel like i
was in a band in the nineties

April 16, 2019 10:56 PM
i have always been the person who got to the
front of the roller coaster line and then changed their
mind and then was talked into riding the front car

April 16, 2019 11:08 PM
productive solitude
productive solitude and the body politic

April 16, 2019 11:18 PM
when i listen to "hotel chelsea #2" i can't tell if
i'm crying for janis or leonard cohen or me

April 16, 2019 11:24 PM
natty said post malone wuldn't be a good
boyfriend but he'd be a committed boyfriend

April 16, 2019 11:26 PM
kendrick would be a good boyfriend probably
chance the rapper would also be a good
boyfriend but he'd love god more than you he would
put god first then chicago then kids then you

April 16, 2019 11:28 PM
natty said you really just have to be kim to date kanye sarah said i say this because i care but you should stop dating rappers maybe

April 16, 2019 11:41 PM
~~hey elliot i like you i do i like that we pronounce gif the same way like "gif" and i like that you know that you should eat something dry with an espresso and i like you but i'm still getting bosco's records delivered to my mailing address and the other day i reached out for the box of ginger snaps in the pantry and i found a singular double stuft oreo left behind from the pack bosco bought and i thought about how he's gone but stupid dumb traces of his presence remain and it feels cheap even though it shouldn't to be moving on and i think i need to not be with him and not be with you and i think i need to be alone i might even want to be alone for the first time in a long time and maybe have meaningless sex with a stranger or not or maybe even just watch duck soup in bed alone with a bag of popcorn chips and let the crumbs fall onto the sheets and not worry about it and maybe you can wait for me or maybe you can't but you certainly don't have to and maybe the truth is that i like you but i just i need a hot second~~

April 16, 2019 11:54 PM
hey elliot i like you i do but i just got another one of his records in the mail and the other day i reached i reached out for the box of ginger snaps

in the pantry and i found a singular double stuffed oreo left behind from the pack bosco bought and i thought about how he's gone but stupid dumb traces of his presence remain and it feels cheap even though it shouldn't to be moving on and i think i need to not be with him and or anyone else right now i think i need to be alone i might even want to be alone for the first time in a long time maybe watch duck soup in bed alone with a bag of popcorn chips and let the crumbs fall onto the sheets and not worry about it and maybe you can wait for me or maybe you can't but you certainly don't have to and maybe the truth is that i like you but i just need a minute

April 17, 2019 7:14 AM
woke to the sound of the needle scratching dead wax and the a/c switched to energy saver mode i turned it off and the quiet felt stark

April 17, 2019 7:15 AM
thought about letting the quiet settle in but i set the needle back on the first groove and let the record play again